Parrot goes to Playschool

Written by Jeanne Willis
Pictures by Mark Birchall

Andersen Press • London

It was Parrot's first day at playschool.
"You'll soon find someone to talk to,"
said the teacher.
And he did.

He went and talked to Guinea Pig.

Guinea Pig was talking to Penguin at the time, but that didn't stop Parrot.

"Hello! My name is Parrot. Where's your tail?
Can you do this with your wings?
Got any brazil nuts?" he said. Very loudly.

Guinea Pig put her fingers in her ears.
"I was talking to Guinea Pig," said Penguin.
"So was I," said Parrot. "I like talking,
don't you?"
But Penguin couldn't get a word in edgeways.

Over in the corner, Python and Puma were playing eye-spy.

"I spy with my little eye something beginning with C!" said Puma.

"Cake," interrupted Parrot.

"I'm supposed to guess, not you," said Python.

"Cauliflower," interrupted Parrot.

"Oh, I was going to say that!" said Python.

And that was the end of that game.

"Storytime..." called the teacher.
Everybody sat on the rug and the teacher
started to read.

"Once upon a time, there was a beautiful..."

"Parrot!" interrupted Parrot.

"...a beautiful princess," said the teacher, "and she lived in a golden..."

"Cage!" yelled Parrot.

"...castle," said the teacher. "One day, a prince rode by in a..."

"Cabbage!" interrupted Parrot.

"...carriage," said the teacher.

"Miss!" said Weasel. "Mi...iss! Parrot keeps interrupting."

"Let's all be very quiet and listen to the story," said the teacher.

"Yes, let's!" said Parrot. "I like stories about Parrots and stories about Pirates and I know a really good one with a parrot *and* a pirate in it…"

And by the time he'd finished, there was no time for the princess story.

It was time for Show and Tell.

Elephant had a little bag of something.

"I'm going to show these," he told Pig. "My mother made them but she used too much sugar and not enough butt..."

"Oooh!" interrupted Parrot. "Are they sweets? Are they nuts? Are they my favourite nutty sweets?"

"No, they're not," said Elephant. "I'm afraid they're very, very..."

But before Elephant could stop him, Parrot had
helped himself to a huge beakful.

Elephant stood up.

"Today for Show and Tell I have a bag of very, very sticky toffees," he said.

And he told everybody how his mother had used too much sugar and not enough butter, and that if anybody tried to eat one of these toffees it would probably stick his beak together.

And, for once, Parrot didn't say a word!